First published by the Blue Sky Press, an Imprint of Scholastic Inc., USA, as
How Do Dinosaurs Learn Their Colors? in 2006 and *How Do Dinosaurs Count to Ten?* in 2004
This edition first published in paperback in Great Britain by HarperCollins Children's Books in 2007

5 7 9 10 8 6

ISBN-13: 978-0-00-724473-7

HarperCollins Children's Books is a division of HarperCollins Publishers Ltd.
Text copyright © Jane Yolen 2004, 2006
Illustrations copyright © Mark Teague 2004, 2006
Visit our website at: www.harpercollins.co.uk
Printed in China by South China Printing Co.Ltd

JANE YOLEN
How Do Dinosaurs Learn Colours and Numbers?

Illustrated by

MARK TEAGUE

HarperCollins *Children's Books*

How Do Dinosaurs Learn Colours?

Dinosaur colours

start with red:

GORGOSAURUS

A **red** fire engine

tucked under the bed,

a **purple** towel
left on the floor,

GALLIMIMUS

a green sign taped

to the bedroom door,

a **blue** robe thrown

across two chairs,

a **pink** ball
bouncing down
the stairs,

ANKYLOSAURUS

yellow bananas

right by a plate,

APATOSAURUS

brown circles

all around a date,

white chalk marks

on an old **black** slate

VELOCIRAPTOR

and an orange backpack –

don't be late!

Rainbows here
and rainbows there...

CRYOLOPHOSAURUS

Dinosaur colours

everywhere!

How Do Dinosaurs Learn Numbers?

Dinosaur counting
starts with one.
One tattered
teddy bear
just for fun.

TYRANNOSAURUS REX

Two big balloons
tied to the bed,

three toy trucks painted

blue, green and red.

Four balls that bounce,

five big letter blocks

and under the bed,
six dirty socks.

A track, an engine

and seven cars,

STEGOSAURUS

an easel with eight

full paint jars.

Nine pictures hanging
on the wall,

ten books to read –
and that is all.

Now that he's counted
from one to ten,
how does
a dinosaur
count again?

APATOSAURUS

AGAIN!

How Do Dinosaurs...

ISBN: 978-0-00-713728-2

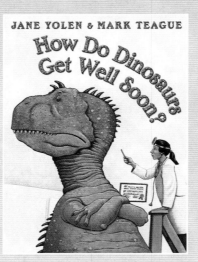

ISBN: 978-0-00-717236-8

ISBN: 978-0-00-721609-3

Board Book
ISBN: 978-0-00-723561-2

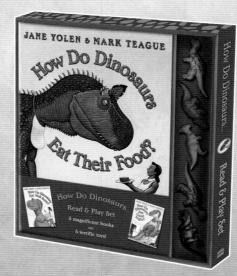

Read and Play Set
ISBN: 978-0-00-724219-1

Collect all the books in this terrific series by Jane Yolen and Mark Teague!